HURRICANE WATCH

MELISSA STEWART · ILLUSTRATED BY TAIA MORLEY

HARPER

An Imprint of HarperCollinsPublishers

Special thanks to Michael J. Brennan, PhD, Meteorologist, for his valuable assistance.

The Let's-Read-and-Find-Out Science book series was originated by Dr. Franklyn M. Branley, Astronomer Emeritus and former Chairman of the American Museum of Natural History–Hayden Planetarium, and was formerly co-edited by him and Dr. Roma Gans, Professor Emeritus of Childhood Education, Teachers College, Columbia University. Text and illustrations for each of the books in the series are checked for accuracy by an expert in the relevant field. For more information about Let's-Read-and-Find-Out Science books, write to HarperCollins Children's Books, 195 Broadway, New York, NY 10007, or visit our website at www.letsreadandfindout.com.

Let's Read-and-Find-Out Science® is a trademark of HarperCollins Publishers.

ISBN 978-0-06-232776-5 (trade bdg.) —ISBN 978-0-06-232775-8 (pbk.)

The artist used watercolor and traditional media with Adobe Photoshop to create the digital illustrations for this book.
Typography by Erica De Chavez
15 16 17 18 19   SCP   10 9 8 7 6 5 4 3 2 1
❖
First Edition

For Gerard, who weathers life's storms
and successes by my side—M.S.

For Tony, my best friend rain or shine—T.M.

"Hurricane watch," says the TV weatherperson.
Scientists at the National Hurricane Center have been
tracking the storm for a week. Now they think it may
strike land in a couple of days. It's time to get ready.

PACIFIC
OCEAN

HURRICANE

SHELTER

10

Some hurricanes form in the Pacific Ocean, but they rarely hit land.

ATLANTIC OCEAN

HURRICANES

Powerful swirling ocean storms in the Western Pacific Ocean are called typhoons.

PACIFIC OCEAN

Most hurricanes form off the coast of Africa.

TYPHOONS

Powerful swirling ocean storms in the Indian Ocean are called cyclones.

CYCLONES

INDIAN OCEAN

N W E S

What is a **hurricane**? It's a huge, powerful spinning storm that moves across the ocean. Most hurricanes form off the west coast of Africa. Then they move west toward the Americas.

·AUGUST·
·SEPTEMBER·
·OCTOBER·

Most hurricanes form in August, September, or October. That's when ocean water is warmest in the northern half of the world.

WATER VAPOR RISES

COOLER AIR RUSHES IN

When air over the ocean heats up, seawater **evaporates**. That means it changes from a liquid into a gas called **water vapor**. Then the water vapor rises up, up into the sky.

As the warm, moist air climbs higher, other air rushes in to take its place. That moving air is what we call wind.

As the wind blows, warm, moist air continues to rise. And as it moves up, it starts to cool.

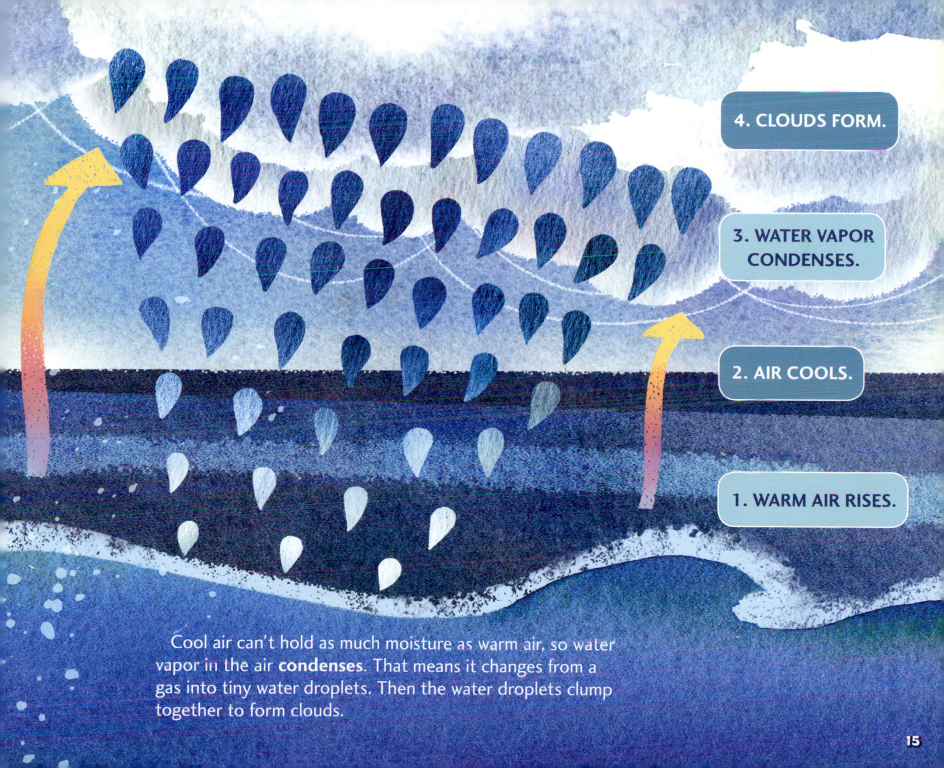

4. CLOUDS FORM.

3. WATER VAPOR CONDENSES.

2. AIR COOLS.

1. WARM AIR RISES.

Cool air can't hold as much moisture as warm air, so water vapor in the air **condenses**. That means it changes from a gas into tiny water droplets. Then the water droplets clump together to form clouds.

As clouds form, the warm air above the ocean rises faster and faster. And that makes the wind stronger and stronger. When wind speeds reach 39 miles per hour, scientists call it a **tropical storm**.

The faster the warm air from the ocean rises, the taller the storm cloud grows.

As Earth moves through space, it spins round and round. That spinning is what makes hurricanes swirl in circles.

The whole storm spins round and round. It rises higher and higher. It spreads wider and wider as it moves across the ocean.

During hurricane season, scientists keep a close eye on storms in the Atlantic Ocean. Satellites in space take pictures day and night.

Sometimes scientists have to watch two or more tropical storms at the same time. Giving the storms names, such as Katrina, Rita, and Wilma, makes them easier to track.

Airplanes fly straight into the storms. They measure how strong a storm is, which way it is headed, and how fast it is moving toward land.

Some tropical storms fizzle out. But others keep on growing bigger and stronger.

When the swirling winds inside a tropical storm reach 74 miles per hour, scientists call it a hurricane. It may be 10 miles high and more than 100 miles wide.

Scientists watch hurricanes very closely. There is no way to stop these superstorms. But knowing when and where a hurricane will strike can help people stay safe.

HURRICANE WATCH!

When a hurricane may hit land in a couple of days, people should:

- ✔ Make sure they have canned foods, bottled drinking water, first-aid supplies, and extra batteries for flashlights and radios.
- ✔ Charge cell-phone batteries.
- ✔ Fill their cars' gas tanks in case they need to leave their homes and drive to safer areas.
- ✔ Bring in chairs and bikes and garbage cans so they won't blow away.

HURRICANE WARNING!

When a hurricane will hit land in a day or so, people should:

- ✔ Listen to the radio or watch TV for news about the storm.
- ✔ Cover their windows with shutters or boards.
- ✔ Go indoors and stay in a safe place away from doors and windows.
- ✔ Leave their homes if the police ask them to.

Sometimes a hurricane dies out.
But if it keeps on sucking up more and
more hot, moist air, it will grow larger
and larger, stronger and stronger.
Winds whip. Waves crash. Rain pours
down. The giant spinning storm moves
closer and closer to land.

When a hurricane hits land, thick clouds
cover the sky. Howling winds are so loud,
they drown out all other sounds.

Rain falls hard and fast. The wind
blows it sideways.

Sometimes trees bend to
the ground. Houses shake.
Windows break. And
roofs fly off into
the air.

Strong winds create a **storm surge** that pushes ocean water toward the shore. Giant waves crash down. The water crushes boats and docks. It can even flood streets and wash away homes.

WEATHER ALERT

Scientists use the Saffir-Simpson scale to rate the strength of hurricane winds.

Category	Wind Speed
1	74–95 miles per hour
2	96–110 miles per hour
3	111–129 miles per hour
4	130–156 miles per hour
5	157+ miles per hour

Then the wind dies down. The rain stops, and the sky turns blue. But the storm isn't over.

The center, or **eye**, of a hurricane is clear and calm. It's an open hole in the middle of the swirling clouds and winds.

After the eye passes, stormy weather returns. The winds whip and even more rain falls.

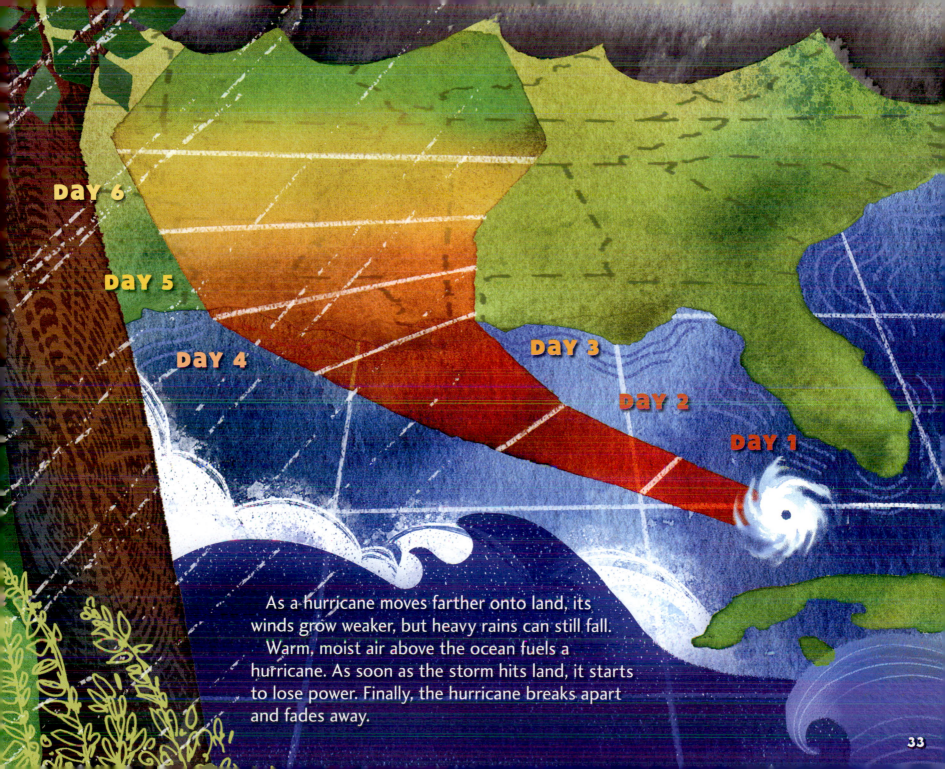

DAY 6

DAY 5

DAY 4

DAY 3

DAY 2

DAY 1

As a hurricane moves farther onto land, its winds grow weaker, but heavy rains can still fall. Warm, moist air above the ocean fuels a hurricane. As soon as the storm hits land, it starts to lose power. Finally, the hurricane breaks apart and fades away.

33

Hurricanes are scary storms.
But thanks to hard-working
scientists, they don't take us
by surprise.

If a hurricane is headed
your way, listen to weather
reports. Follow directions from
police. These people will tell
you how to stay safe.

GLOSSARY

Condense—to change from a gas to a liquid

Evaporate—to change from a liquid to a gas

Eye (of a hurricane)—the clear, calm center of a hurricane

Hurricane—a powerful, rotating ocean storm on either side of the Americas with winds of at least 74 miles per hour

Storm surge—the rise of ocean water caused by a tropical storm or hurricane

Tropical storm—A rotating ocean storm with winds between 39 and 73 miles per hour. A tropical storm can turn into a hurricane, a cyclone, or a typhoon depending on where it is in the world.

Water vapor—the gas form of water

FIND OUT MORE ABOUT HURRICANES
Activities to Try

Going Up!

We can't see air, so how do we know that warm air rises? To find out, you will need a 6- x 6-inch piece of construction paper, scissors, a 4-inch piece of string, and a lamp with the shade removed.

1. Cut the paper into a spiraling line like the shape of a snail's shell.
2. Tie a knot in one end of the string.
3. Poke a small hole in the top of the paper spiral and pull the string through.
4. Turn on the lightbulb, hold the paper spiral above it, and watch what happens.

The lightbulb heats the air around it. As the warm air rises, it makes the paper spiral spin.

Fast and Fierce

Which part of a hurricane has the strongest winds? To find out, you will need a paper clip, a 10-inch piece of string, a large bowl, water, and a wooden spoon.

1. Tie the paper clip to the string.
2. Add water to the bowl until it is about three-quarters full.
3. Using the wooden spoon, stir the water round and round.
4. Dip the paper clip in various parts of the spinning water. Where does it circle the fastest?

The water in the bowl moves just like the wind inside a hurricane. It is strongest just outside the central eye.

WEBSITES TO VISIT

NATIONAL HURRICANE CENTER
www.nhc.noaa.gov
Track tropical storms as they move
across the Atlantic Ocean.

HURRICANE HUNTERS
www.hurricanehunters.com
Learn about the brave scientists that
fly straight into hurricanes.

HURRICANES
www.miamisci.org/hurricane
Watch a video of a
hurricane in progress.

Be sure to look for all of these books in the **Let's-Read-and-Find-Out Science** series: